Mary and Jo, thanks for your inspiration!
~ Julia

BOYS TOWN® Press

Boys Town, Nebraska

Written by **Julia Cook**

Illustrated by Anita DuFalla

Decibella and her 6-inch VOICE

Decibella and Her 6-inch Voice

ISBN 978-1-934490-58-7

Published by the Boys Town Press
13603 Flanagan Blvd.
Boys Town, NE 68010

For a Boys Town Press catalog, call **1-800-282-6657**
or visit our website: **BoysTownPress.org**

Publisher's Cataloging-in-Publication Data

Cook, Julia, 1964-

Decibella and her 6-inch voice / written by Julia Cook ; illustrated by Anita DuFalla. -- Boys Town, NE : Boys Town Press, c2014.

p. ; cm.
(Communicate with confidence; 2nd)

ISBN: 978-1-934490-58-7

Audience: K-6th grade.
Summary: Isabella enjoys shouting out her thoughts, ideas and feelings so much, it's earned her the nickname "Decibella!". Young readers will be entertained as she learns the "five volumes" of voice-- whisper, 6-inch, table-talk, strong speaker, and outside-- and that different situations require a different tone.--Publisher.

1. Oral communication--Juvenile fiction. 2. Loudness--Juvenile fiction. 3. Conversation--Juvenile fiction. 4. Etiquette for children and teenagers--Juvenile fiction. 5. Interpersonal communication in children--Juvenile fiction. 6. Interpersonal relations in children--Juvenile fiction. 7. Social interaction in children--Juvenile fiction. 8. Children--Language--Juvenile fiction. 9. Children--Life skills guides. 10. [Oral communication--Fiction. 11. Loudness--Fiction. 12. Conversation--Fiction. 13. Etiquette--Fiction. 14. Interpersonal communication--Fiction. 15. Interpersonal relations--Fiction. 16. Behavior--Fiction. 17. Conduct of life.] I. DuFalla, Anita. II. Title. III. Series: Communicate with confidence ; no. 2.

PZ7.C76984 D43 2014

[E]--dc23 1403

Printed in the United States
10 9 8 7 6

Boys Town Press is the publishing division of Boys Town, a national organization serving children and families.

My name is **Isabella**...
but sometimes people call me

Decibella,

and I have

no idea why.

I like the name Isabella much better.

“I’m done with my test!”

“SHHH, Decibella, SHHHH!”

"Do you have any books about squirrel monkeys?"

"SHHH, Decibella, SHHHH!"

"MOM, I'm home!"

"SHHH, Decibella, SHHHH!"

"Hi, Grandma!"
"SHHH, Decibella, SHHHH!"
"I'll have the Smiley Face pancakes!"
"SHHHHHHHH!"
TINA
PANCAKE PALACE
PANCAKE PALACE

Isn't that one of YOUR STUDENTS?
"Pass the popcorn PLEASE!"
"SHHHHHHHHH!"

Today, my teacher asked me to stay in for recess so we could have a little chat.

"Isabella, I'm proud of you for doing so well on your social studies test. And your book report on squirrel monkeys was one of the very best!

But today we need to talk about how to make a better choice. Sometimes you talk way too loud, and you need to lower your voice.

It's important that you speak loud enough for those who need to hear. But you don't want to speak so loud that people cover their ears.

It kinda bugs others when your voice is

way too loud.

Sometimes you need to

talk softer,

and I can show you how."

"Most of the time when we are working in the classroom, you need to use your 6-inch Voice."

"What's that?"

"Your 6-inch Voice is halfway between your Whisper Voice and your Table-Talk Voice."

"My what?"

"Isabella, you have ***Five Voice Volumes,*** *and you get to decide which one works best for you and others when you're trying to get things done.*

"SLURPADO

There's Whisper, 6-inch, Table-Talk, Strong Speaker, *and* Outside. *Let's use the word* 'SLURPADOODLE' *and give each of them a try."*

"Slurpawhatta?"

Strong Speaker

ODLE!”

"Let's start in the middle.

Say 'SLURPADOODLE' in your Table-Talk voice. That's the voice that I'm using now. It's your regular talking voice."

"Slurpadoodle."

"This is the voice you will use the most.
It's how people talk on TV.
It's not too loud, and it's not too soft.
It's as regular as can be!

Use your Table-Talk voice when you are hanging out with your friends at the mall, talking on the phone, or talking to others at the dinner table."

"Now shout 'SLURPADOODLE' as loud as you can."

"SLURPADOODLE!"

"This is what your Outside Voice *sounds like.*
You can hear it from far away.
Use it to cheer on your team at a game,
or when you go outside to play."

"When you bring your Outside Voice inside, it gets you into trouble. Unless, of course, you have an emergency and you need to call for help. Like last week, when you accidentally got your hair caught in the door!"

"Now, find the voice that is halfway between your Table-Talk Voice and your Outside Voice, and use it to say 'SLURPADOODLE.'"

"Slurpadoodle!"

"This is your Strong Speaker Voice.

Your Strong Speaker Voice
is the voice that you use
when you need to talk to a group.
You need to breathe in deep, stand up tall,
speak strong, and try not to stoop."

Strong Speaker

"Use your Strong Speaker Voice when you need to be a speaker, like when you are giving an oral report in class or acting in a play."

"Now, let's go back to the middle again…

Say 'SLURPADOODLE' in your Table-Talk voice."

"Slurpadoodle."

"Perfect!"

"Now whisper 'SLURPADOODLE.'"

"Slurpadoodle."

"Isabella, this is what your Whisper Voice *sounds like.*
It's the softest voice you can make.
You have to be right next to the people you're talking to,
or they cannot hear what you say."

Whisper Voice

"Use your Whisper Voice when you're trying to be quiet in the library, when you need to ask me a question during a test, or when you're in a movie theatre and you need to talk but you don't want to bother other people around you who are trying to watch the show."

6-inch

"Now find your voice that's halfway between your Table-Talk Voice and your Whisper Voice, and use it to say 'SLURPADOODLE.'"

"Slurpadoodle!"

"This is your 6-inch Voice!!!! That means if a person is more than six inches away from you, he can't hear your voice."

"Six inches is about the distance
from your pinky to your thumb.
So place your thumb on your chin like this
and see if we can have some fun!"

"Can you hear me now???"

"Can you hear me now???"

"Can you hear me now???"

"Most of the time when you are working in class, I need you to use your 6-inch voice."

"When everyone uses their 6-inch voice, *our classroom starts to* BUZZ!
Nobody makes too much noise, and our work gets done because...

We can talk and work, and still stay on track. And our voices don't bug each other.
A BUZZING *classroom sings*

'GUESS WHAT? We're working with one another!'"

?

"Isabella, you're in charge of how loud you are.
You get to control your own voice.
And now that you are a voice volume expert,
I know you can make the right choice!"

"I'm done with my assignment."

"Thank you, Isabella, for using your 6-inch Voice while we are working in the classroom."

"Do you have any books about three-toed sloths?"

"Thank you, Isabella, for using your Whisper Voice in the library."

"My report today is about the planet Mars!"

"Isabella, I love the way you used your Strong Speaker Voice when you gave your oral report!"

"Hi, Grandma!"

"Hi, Isabella, it's so great to hear your voice!"

"I just love it when I can be as loud as I want!!!!"

"Now that I'm a voice expert,
I think about what voice to use.
My 6-inch Voice *works best in class,*
but when I'm outside, I get to choose."

"I never bring my Outside Voice *inside because it's way too loud, unless I'm at a basketball game, and I'm cheering with the crowd."*

Strong Speaker

Outside

"Now other kids don't call me Decibella, because I know what voice to use. There's Whisper, 6-inch, Table Talk, Strong Speaker *and* Outside –

I get to choose!"

"Of course,
I can use my Outside Voice *inside*
if there's a need for urgency.
Like last week when I caught
my hair in the door.
Now that was a true
EMERGENCY!"

Boys Town Press Books by Julia Cook

Kid-friendly titles to teach social skills

A book series to help kids master the art of communicating.

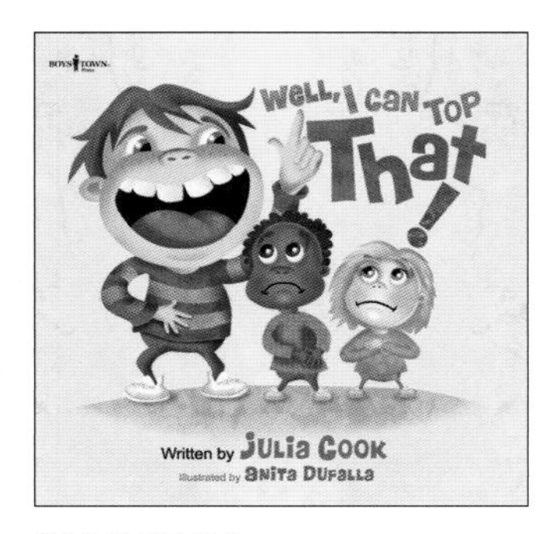

978-1-934490-57-0

978-1-934490-76-1

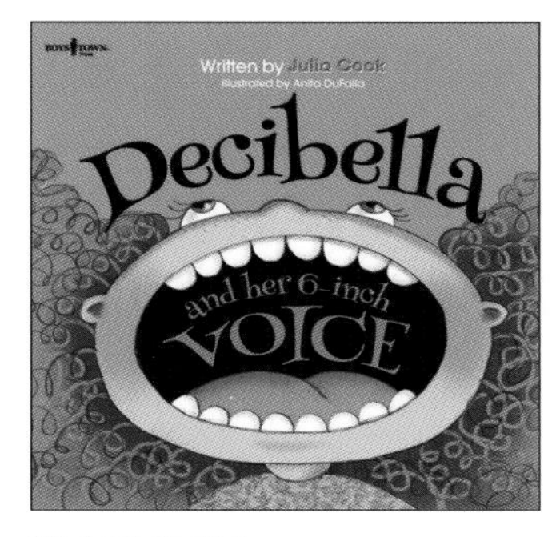

978-1-934490-58-7

978-1-944882-13-6

NEW TITLES

A book series to help kids get along.

Making Friends is An Art!
Cliques Just Don't Make Cents
Tease Monster
Peer Pressure Gauge
Hygiene...You Stink!
I Want to Be the Only Dog
The Judgmental Flower
Table Talk
Rumor Has It...

A book series to help kids take responsibility for their behaviors.

But It's Not My Fault
Baditude!
The Procrastinator
Cheaters Never Prosper
That Rule Doesn't Apply to Me!
What's in It for Me?

Reinforce the social skills RJ learns in each book.

The Worst Day of My Life Ever!
el PEOR día de TODA mi vida
I Just Don't Like the Sound of NO!
¡No me gusta cómo se oye NO!
Sorry, I Forgot to Ask!
I Just Want to Do It My Way!
Teamwork Isn't My Thing, and I Don't Like to Share!
Thanks for the Feedback... (I Think!)
I Can't Believe You Said That!

Tips for Parents and Educators

JULIA COOK
Because Kids Don't Come With Instructions.

Some kids seem to have only two volumes: **LOUD** and **LOUDER**. Parents and educators are in charge of teaching kids proper voice volume, but there are some things that must be understood in order to make that teaching as effective as possible. If a child speaks too loudly, it is important to identify the reasons why:

- Children who are hard of hearing often speak louder in order to hear themselves. It is important to consult a physician in order to rule this out and/or seek treatment.
- Some kids who feel ignored when speaking will increase their voice volume to get attention.
- Some kids need to be the center of attention, so they talk loudly.
- Some kids become louder when they are tired or hungry, or when other physical needs are not being met.
- Some kids are just naturally loud.

Whatever the reason, it is important to remember that each child is unique and may require individual attention when teaching proper voice volume. Here are a few strategies that can help:

1. **Teach and model the five voice volumes** (Whisper, 6-inch, Table-Talk, Strong Speaker, and Outside) and practice each level at appropriate places, such as in the yard, at the library, in the lunchroom, and in the car.
2. **Offer small rewards** when kids use the right voice volume at the right time.
3. **When a child is speaking loudly for attention,** show that you hear what is being said by establishing eye contact and quietly restating the words back to her without getting angry.
4. **Whisper.** Whispering will get kids' attention because it makes them curious. Kids always want to know if there's a secret. Whispering will get a child's attention much more effectively than yelling.
5. **If a child often tries to be the center of attention by speaking loudly,** he may have strong character and leadership abilities that need to be channeled and developed as strengths.
6. **Prepare ahead of time.** Kids will often get louder when they are bored. If you are planning to take a long car ride, go to the library, or dine at a restaurant, take along a few activities, games, or snacks.
7. **Use a voice meter.** Kids sometimes have to see how loud they are in order to hear how loud they are.
8. **Offer outlets where kids can be loud.** Make sure you give kids the opportunity to be as loud as they want and need to be at times throughout the day. Kids are full of energy, and they need to be able to release that energy. Teaching kids to do this at the right times and places requires that you provide those times and places.
9. **Promote proper nutrition and use calming bedtime routines.**
10. **Remember, all children are unique** and some kids are naturally louder than others. What works for one child may not work for every child, so be willing to try different strategies.
11. **It is important to remember that using appropriate voice volume is a learned behavior**. The most effective way to teach proper voice volume is to model it effectively and consistently.

For more parenting information, visit boystown.org/parenting.